W9-AVL-787

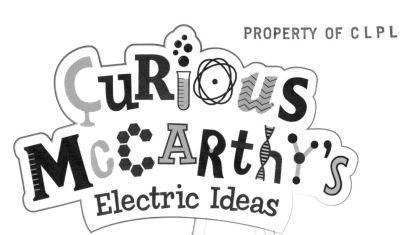

CuRioUS McCARthY's
Electric Ideas

by Tory Christie   illustrated by Mina Price

PICTURE WINDOW BOOKS
a capstone imprint

Curious McCarthy is published by Picture Window Books,
A Capstone Imprint
1710 Roe Crest Drive
North Mankato, Minnesota 56003
www.mycapstone.com

Cataloging-in-Publication Data is available on the Library of Congress website.
ISBN: 978-1-5158-1644-7 (library binding)
ISBN: 978-1-5158-1648-5 (paperback)
ISBN: 978-1-5158-1652-2 (eBook PDF)

Summary: When the power goes out at the McCarthy home, young scientist
Curious McCarthy becomes more interested in electricity. Unfortunately, her
mischievous brother is showing interest too, and Curious is certain that will
lead to trouble.

Designer: Ashlee Suker

Printed and bound in Canada.
010382F17

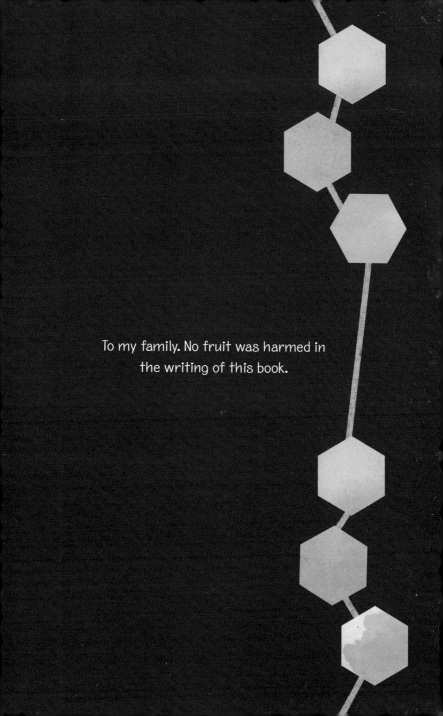

To my family. No fruit was harmed in
the writing of this book.

The McCarthys

CURIOUS (age 10) Scientist, arm wrestler, and battery expert.

ANNE (age 11) Comedi[an], arm wrestler, and name[d] after another dead auth[or].

JOHN GLENN (age 8) Notice the age gap between John Glenn and the rest of the boys? That should tell you something . . . he is a lot of work.

BENJAMIN (age 5) The family member with no sense of humor.

EDISON (age 4) The youngest McCarthy with lots of questions.

MRS. STICKLER (age 103) Homeroom teacher.

MS. FICKLEBY (age 203) Reading teacher with lips that are never zipped.

RANDY STUDLEY Last year's arm-wrestling champ. But will he win this year?

MILY (age 12) Mature, but weird, d named after a dead author.

CHARLOTTE (age 13) Prim, proper, and named after a dead author.

MOM English professor with a love of books – and no decorating abilities.

DAD A thrifty man with a great imagination and a thing for used toothbrushes.

MR. CORNFORTH A principal with a baby-like scream.

MR. SWETT PE teacher and Navy SEAL with a baby-like scream.

MR. SNORTLAND Fragrant substitute teacher.

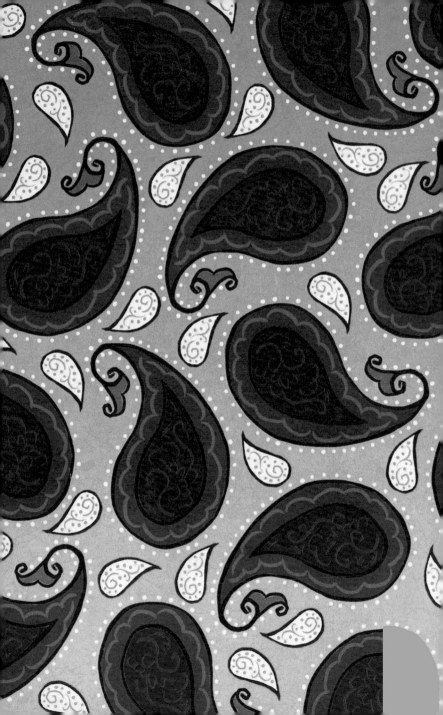

1

Sunday, 4:00 p.m.

You have to use your imagination when you have a
large, thrifty family.[1]

We have one TV. We have one computer. And on
this particular Sunday, we had no power. That meant
no TV. No computer. No lights. And the board games
were all in the basement.

Our basement is creepy. No one goes down there
without lights. Except for Dad. He had to check the
breaker box.[2]

---

1   This is a footnote. Some of you already know about footnotes. For those who don't,
footnotes clarify information. Thrifty is a word that means the McCarthys are cheap. We
do not have a lot of money, so we have to use it wisely. That sometimes takes a great
deal of imagination. Like how to reuse an old toothbrush or Easy-Bake Oven.
2   A breaker box is where the electricity comes into a house. Or a building or a
school . . . I guess.

"There's nothing to do," said my brother John Glenn.

"Go outside and play," said Mom. She was happily sitting by a window and reading a book.[3]

"It's colder than Alaska during a snowstorm!" said my sister Emily. Actually, it wasn't nearly that cold, but Emily is no scientist.

"There must be something you can all do," said Dad, coming up from the basement. "Use your imaginations!" Most parents want kids to use their imagination. But the McCarthys have a lot of crazy ideas. Dad was inviting trouble, if you ask me.

What can seven kids do when they are stuck inside the house on a cold day with no power? Plenty . . . apparently.

Edison was dragging his feet across the carpet. When he reached Charlotte, he touched her elbow.

"OUCH!" she shouted. "Edison, you shocked me!"

---

3   It was *Frankenstein*, just in case you are curious.

Edison laughed. Suddenly John Glenn and Benjamin were dragging their feet across the floor. They held out their fingers and shocked each other, trying for a bigger shock each time.

"Look at that!" said Dad. "The electricity may be out, but the boys decided to make their own electricity. They are moving electrons! Now that's using your imaginations!"[4]

---

4   Electrons are parts of atoms. Atoms make up everything: for example, rocks, trees, people, socks, and little brothers.

Anne and I slipped off our shoes. We pushed back two purple chairs. That gave us more room to drag our stocking feet across the carpet.

We looked at the carpet under where the chairs had been. I observed three centimeters of dust, two pennies, and one orange toothbrush. Anne and I each grabbed a penny and left the rest. We could not be expected to vacuum with no electricity, right?

Dad grabbed the toothbrush. He said, "You never know when this might come in handy!"[5]

Anne and I joined the three boys and tried to make bigger and bigger shocks by touching one another. John Glenn's hair was sticking up. That was from the static electricity. I looked at Anne. Her long hair was in a ponytail. It didn't stick up.

---

5   The McCarthys are thrifty, but saving an old, crusty toothbrush is a little too much.

I shuffled past a mirror. My hair is on the messy side on an average day. But today it was wild. A few hairs were standing straight up from my scalp.

"That's an attractive look, Curious," said Charlotte.

Charlotte and Emily didn't join in with our static game. They are both in middle school, which means that they are too mature for static electricity.

You are probably wondering about our large family. I have three older sisters. They are Charlotte, Emily, and Anne. They are named after the Brontë sisters who are three dead authors.[6]

I used to wonder why I wasn't named after a famous author too. It turns out that when I was born, the family plan went wrong. After three girls in a row, my parents thought for sure they would finally have a boy.

---

6   You probably have never heard of the Brontë sisters. They wrote some books that you won't want to read until you are at least in high school – so don't worry about that now.

They had a deal before they got married. Mom, who is an English professor, got to name the girls after famous authors. Dad, who is a mechanical engineer, got to name the boys. He wanted to name them after engineers and inventors and stuff like that.

When I showed up instead of a boy, Dad got a little worried that he might get stuck with all girls. So he got to name me. He named me Curie after Madame Marie Curie. But everyone calls me Curious.

Fortunately for Dad, my three brothers came along. My brothers are John Glenn, Benjamin, and Edison. You might be able to figure out who they were named after.[7]

That is enough about my family. Let's get back to me. I am a scientist. As a scientist, I make observations and do research. I knew that lightning had something to do with electricity. But how did the storm make the lights go out?

----
7 Just in case you can't, that information is in Chapter Two.

Did it have something to do with the breaker box? I wondered just how light bulbs and electricity worked.

As I watched John Glenn drag his feet across the carpet, I saw in his eyes that he had some ideas about electricity too. Sometimes scientists make hypotheses. Hypotheses are basically guesses. Here is my latest hypothesis:

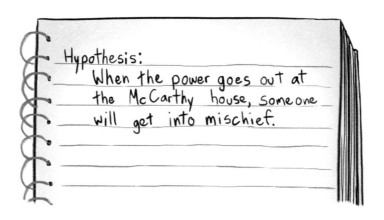

Hypothesis:
When the power goes out at the McCarthy house, someone will get into mischief.

And by someone, I mean John Glenn.

2

It started getting dark. Mom gave up on her reading. She walked to the kitchen. I observed a sock stuck to the back of her sweater. That was static electricity in action.

Lightning struck and the lights in the house flickered on for a second. But then they flickered out. After the lightning, we counted: one-one-thousand, two-one-thousand. BOOM! That meant the lightning strike must have been two miles away. At least according to Mom and Dad.[8]

----

8   Mom and Dad were wrong. Most scientists say that you should divide your count by five to tell you how many miles it is to the lightning strike. So the lightning is probably closer. But what if I want to use the metric system? Should I count faster?

"How am I going to do my homework?" asked Charlotte.

"Where is the flashlight?" said Emily.

"The flashlight is in the kitchen, but the batteries are dead," said Anne.

"Don't worry about homework for now," said Dad.

"Yes," said Mom. She walked in from the kitchen with a candle. "We can have some fun!"

I wondered how being stuck in a dark house with your parents and six brothers and sisters was going to be fun. I settled in to observe.

"We can play games," said Mom.

"Like Baloney!" said Emily. Baloney happens to be her favorite game. That's because she always wins. And that's because she made it up.

I wasn't sure how we would play in the dark. Baloney is a game where you write fake definitions for really funny words.[9]

---

9   Like "bunkum" and "drivel." I am not going to tell you what those words mean. Look them up.

"Let's play telephone!" Dad said. "We can play that in the dark."

We all sat in a circle. Dad started by saying a sentence into Charlotte's ear. She whispered it to Emily, then Emily whispered to Anne, then Anne to me. Then I whispered in John Glenn's ear, then John Glenn to Ben, then Ben to Edison, then Edison to Mom.[10]

Dad explained the rules for the three boys. Each person could say the sentence only once. That meant you had to listen very carefully. Listening carefully is kind of hard if you get stuck next to one of the boys and the whisper is mixed with a little spit.[11]

We played a few rounds of telephone. Dad said, "Einstein loved quantum theory." Leave it to Dad to make this into a learning opportunity.

---

10   So, just in case you haven't figured it out yet, my brother John Glenn is named after the famous astronaut. Ben is named after Benjamin Franklin – who did not discover lightning or electricity by the way, but I'll get to that later. And Edison is named after Thomas Edison, who invented the light bulb. But I don't know how any of this helps now that we have no working light bulbs.

11   By the way, Alexander Graham Bell invented the telephone. And, no, I don't have a brother by that name, but if the McCarthys had eight kids, I bet I would.

We whispered around the circle until Mom said, "I said want a kiwi?"

Dad looked disappointed. Everyone else laughed.

It was Charlotte's turn. She said, "I am very pretty." By the time that got around the circle it turned into "I have to go potty."

The game didn't get much better. John Glenn took his turn. He wanted to go in the other direction. He whispered into my ear. "Thomas Edison invented the light while eating jelly tarts."

I whispered to Anne. Anne whispered to Emily and so on until it got around to Edison.

At some point, the giggling started. I wondered what was so funny about jelly tarts.

Edison doesn't really know how to whisper. He leaned towards Ben. We all heard him say, "Thomas Edison invented the light while eating smelly farts."[12]

----
12   Please don't show this to your teacher. There are some words that you can't say in a kids' book.

John Glenn rolled on the floor laughing. Anne rolled her eyes.

None of the rest of us would have dared to say that word out loud. Our parents are pretty strict about language.

We all looked at Mom and Dad. I wondered what they would do. Then the lights came back on.

"Time to get ready for dinner!" Mom said as she moved toward the kitchen. And so that was some evidence in favor of my hypothesis. John Glenn did get into mischief. But neither John Glenn nor Edison got into trouble for it.

Mom walked into the kitchen as if John Glenn hadn't tricked Edison into saying a bad word. The sock was still stuck to the back of her sweater.

3

The next morning, I looked around Mrs. Stickler's fourth-grade classroom. I wondered if the school had lost power during the storm too.

I studied my surroundings. There were nine large lights on the ceiling. The lights shone down on twenty-two desks. The twenty-two desks sat on a puke green carpet.

The carpet wasn't the plush kind like at home. I wondered if you could make static electricity by dragging your socks on this carpet. Of course, Mrs. Stickler would never let us take off our shoes to try.

My gaze traveled up from the carpet to the desk next to mine. Randy Studley's desk. I studied something hanging from Randy's nose. Then he turned and looked at me. He smiled. Oh great.

That smile did not mean he was looking for a friend. Randy sometimes picks on kids . . . but what he should be picking is his nose. I quickly turned away and looked out the windows.

I noticed the power lines in the distance. I wondered if the school had a breaker box just like we did at home. And if it did and the power went out, who went to check the breaker box? Was it the principal? Did the school even have a basement?

I came up with a whole list of other questions. Scientists like to ask questions.

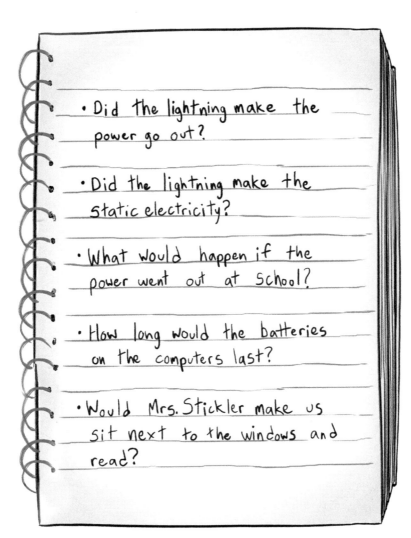

- Did the lightning make the power go out?

- Did the lightning make the static electricity?

- What would happen if the power went out at school?

- How long would the batteries on the computers last?

- Would Mrs. Stickler make us sit next to the windows and read?

Monday, 1:15 p.m.

I am in Mrs. Stickler's fourth-grade homeroom, but I go to a different class for reading. I go to a third-grade reading class with Ms. Fickleby. That's how they do things at this school. It is kind of embarrassing, actually. Especially since John Glenn, who is in second grade, is also in Ms. Fickleby's reading class.

Everyone thinks John Glenn is a really good reader for a second grader. I think that he is just good at tricking people. I needed to keep my eye on him. Maybe I could learn a thing or two.

We were in Ms. Fickleby's reading class when there was an announcement from Principal Cornforth.

"Good afternoon, children," said Mr. Cornforth over the loudspeaker. "It is time again for the annual arm-wrestling contest!" Every year at Hilltop Elementary, the third, fourth, and fifth grades have a contest in the gym.

Randy leaned my way. "I won last year, Curious. Do you want to try to beat me?" He smiled.

"No thanks," I said.

I was NOT going to be in the arm-wrestling contest if it meant I might have to arm wrestle Randy Studley. That would mean I would have to touch his hand. The hand that he probably uses to pick his nose.

The contest would be in front of the whole school in the middle of the gym. The classes would pour into the bleachers. All the students would watch as each kid tried to beat the next one.

"This year we have a special prize for the winner," continued Mr. Cornforth. "The winner will get to be principal for the day. The best arm wrestler will get to follow me around school on my rounds at Hilltop Elementary. Good luck!"

That gave me an idea. If I was principal for a day, I could see if the school had a basement and a breaker box. Maybe it would help me figure out how electricity works.

I changed my mind. I had to win that arm-wrestling contest. The prize was too good.

"I am going to win that contest," said John Glenn.

"Second graders are not allowed," I said.

"Just you wait and see," he said.

"Randy Studley looks pretty strong," I told him. We both looked over to where Randy was joking with his friends.

"Wait and see!" John Glenn laughed.

"See what?" I asked. I might be able to win that contest, but I would need to think like John Glenn. He gets away with everything, and everything goes his way.

I thought for a minute. John Glenn was giving me more evidence for my hypothesis. Well, kind of. He was probably going to get into mischief — but the lights weren't out anymore. Maybe the lights going out at home set this mischief into action — a chain reaction.

"I have a plan," said John Glenn.

"Zip the lips!" said Ms. Fickleby. "It is time to line up for the library."

That was the end of the conversation. I could only wonder about John Glenn's plan. I couldn't ask, because my lips were zipped.

Monday, 1:30 p.m.

The back corner of the library is my laboratory where I can do some research. It happens to be the nonfiction section. Like lots of scientists, I like to work alone. That's why I usually hang out by myself in the library.[13]

Using my usual library tactic, I walked casually toward the shelves with the rest of the class. When I reached the back wall, I crouched down. I snuck behind the shelves to the nonfiction section. Then I crawled along the floor to the 530s.[14]

---

13 It makes sense to hang out by yourself in the library, because there's no talking in the library. Unless you are a librarian. They never have to follow the no-talking-rule.

14 This is a reference to the Dewey Decimal System. The system is a secret code that libraries use to organize their books. The 530s include books on electricity. I was beginning to crack the code.

I spied John Glenn with a stack of books at the end of a row of nonfiction. He glanced my way and slipped around the corner and out of sight.

I looked through the books on the shelf. I saw: *Magnets, Monsters, and Mummies . . . What's the Attraction? . . . Maglev Trains.*

Not exactly what I was looking for, so I looked to the right. I saw books on chemistry. I looked to the left. I saw books on spacecraft. I wanted to know how lights worked. But most of the electricity books must have been checked out.

I spotted a book called *How Conductors Work* and pulled it off the shelf.[15]

As I paged through it, I learned that electrons move around freely in conductors. Water is a conductor. And people are about sixty percent water. That is why people are good conductors. And I guess that is why electrons can move through them.

I took the book and wandered around a bit more. I spotted a book called *Fruity and Freaky Batteries.*

---

15   Conductors are metals or other materials that can conduct electricity. They could also be the person that leads a band or drives a train, but that is not what we are talking about here.

It was tucked in the 640s with the nutrition books. I was pretty sure the book was in the wrong place. No one would eat a fruity battery. But that fruity book might answer some of my electricity questions.

Next I thought about going to find some books on arm wrestling, but the librarian shouted, "Time to line up!"[16]

I settled on *How Conductors Work* and *Fruity and Freaky Batteries*. As we were waiting to check out, I turned to look behind me. There was John Glenn. As soon as he saw me looking, he slipped his books behind his back. What was he hiding?

I wrapped my arms around my own books so he couldn't see the titles. Even though I didn't know what he was up to, I didn't want to give him any more ideas.

---

16   It is a scientific fact that librarians and teachers can't be quiet in the library.

6

Monday, 2:10 p.m.

I was sitting in homeroom later that day, when I smelled something funny. Something like rotting fruit. Or maybe Mrs. Stickler got some new hand sanitizer.[17]

I took a look at her desk. Nope. The same gigantic bottle sat right there on top.

I looked around. I could see other people sniffing too. Even Mrs. Stickler seemed to be sniffing.

She got up from her desk and went to the door. She looked up and down the hall.

----
17 Teachers use a lot of hand sanitizer. That's because they are terrified of germs!

She walked back in the classroom, shutting the door behind her. She walked over and opened one of the windows.

We shivered for the next ten minutes as we worked on a social studies worksheet. I suppose Mrs. Stickler felt bad for us, because she said, "You can all line up to go to music a little early today."

As soon as we walked out into the hall, I smelled that rotten fruity smell again. It got stronger and stronger. When we reached the music classroom, Mrs. Stickler peered through the door.

"Oh, I thought you might be subbing today," she said to someone inside the classroom. She turned to us. "Class, Mr. Snortland is your substitute for music today. Be on your best behavior." With that, she turned and walked away.

Mr. Snortland invited us in. He was a happy guy. The fruity smell got even stronger. It must have been his aftershave.[18]

He had us each place a chair in a circle. I wondered if we were going to play the telephone game. But he had us face the chairs outward. Then he removed one.

"Today, we are going to play musical chairs," Mr. Snortland said with a big smile.

----
18   Aftershave is like perfume. Except it's for men. Apparently aftershave is quite a bit stinkier than perfume.

Apparently he thought that we were the kindergarten class.

There were twenty-one chairs. There were twenty-two kids. I think you know where this is going.

Next he picked a song from the music stand and sat at the piano.

"It's the electric slide!" he shouted and started banging away at the keys.

We stared at him for a minute.

"GO! GO! GO!" he shouted over the piano.

We scurried around the chairs just like a dog chases its tail. Mr. Snortland played faster. We scurried faster.

"Boogie woogie!" he sang.

Mr. Snortland suddenly stopped. Every kid made a mad dash for a chair.

I quickly sat in the closest chair, just edging out Emma Delaney. She leaped into the next chair. That left Paige Pamook. She was the last one standing.

She was out. Mr. Snortland had her sit down on the floor next to the wall.

A light bulb went on in my head.[19]

The kids were like electrons. The circle of chairs was the center of an atom. We scurried around the circle, just like electrons move around the center of an atom. Except there was an extra electron. The extra electron was not going to find a spot on this atom.

Mr. Snortland had everyone except Paige get up. Then he took away one more chair. He started banging the piano again. Each time I came around the circle near the piano, I had to hold my breath.

"Boogie woogie woogie!" sang Mr. Snortland.

After a while, we were down to eight chairs and nine kids. The music stopped. The kids scrambled for empty chairs.

---

19 Not really. That's an idiom. And idiom is a group of words that don't mean what they seem like they mean. There was no light bulb in my head. I had an idea. What I mean is: I think I know how electrons work.

Randy and I were standing next to each other —
with no open chair. I saw an open chair on the
opposite side of the circle. I ran one way. Randy
ran the other.

We both went to sit in the chair at the same time.

We were two electrons fighting for one spot on an atom. Unfortunately, he was a little quicker. He got to the chair right before me. And I ended up sitting on his lap! The entire class laughed. Talk about embarrassment.

Having Randy beat me at musical chairs only made me more determined. I was going to beat him at arm wrestling. I was going to win that contest. I was going to be principal for the day.

Monday, 5:00 p.m.

"Let's practice!" said Dad. He cleared chopped asparagus from the table. John Glenn had told Dad about the arm-wrestling contest, and Dad wanted to show us his technique.[20]

Dad went over the logical way to arm wrestle. With Dad, there is a logical way to do everything.

"You've got to think about the proper angle between your bicep and forearm," Dad said.[21]

---

20 Technique is just a fancy word for style. It is the *way* you perform a task. Technique can be very important in scientific practices too. I was paying close attention, because I am a good scientist – and because I had to learn how to arm wrestle.

21 The bicep is the muscle in the part of your arm that is above the elbow. The forearm is the part of your arm that is below your elbow. I was going to need more than biceps and forearms to win this wrestling contest.

"Why?" asked Edison.

"Because arm wrestling is not about strength. It's about technique," said Dad.

"Why?" asked Edison.

"If John Glenn uses the right technique, he will be able to beat a fifth grader," said Dad.

"But second graders can't be in the contest," I said. "It's against the rules."

"Well, John Glenn can practice for next year," Dad said. "And the right technique can help you girls beat someone who may be a lot bigger or stronger too."

I perked up when Dad said that. I wondered if Randy Studley knew about technique.

Dad demonstrated. Then he had us kids practice while he went back to the stove.

Dad continued to talk about the proper way to arm wrestle as he cooked. I beat John Glenn. But Anne beat me. Maybe because I was distracted by Dad's cooking. The pan he was using had a different metal at the bottom than on the sides. It made me wonder why.

As Anne and John Glenn continued to practice their arm-wrestling technique, I opened *How Conductors Work.* It turns out that copper is a good conductor for electricity. It is also a good conductor for heat, so it is sometimes used on the bottom of kitchen pans.

I hadn't noticed our copper-bottomed pots before. Hopefully, John Glenn doesn't figure this out. He might try to make pennies out of them.[22]

Anne beat John Glenn. I wanted to see if I could beat her using my left arm this time. I am left-handed. That probably means that I am left-armed too.

"You have to use your right arm, Curious," said Anne. Using my right arm might make it extra hard to win the contest. As I was thinking about the possibilities, I looked over at John Glenn. He was looking through my *Conductors* book with a smile on his face. Maybe he had read the part about copper being a good conductor. Maybe he had noticed the pans. Maybe he was making plans to melt the pans to make pennies. What was he thinking?

The kitchen was starting to fill up with hungry McCarthys. My brothers and sisters scrambled around the table. Everyone looked for a good seat.

---

22   Pennies actually haven't been made from copper since 1897. They are now mostly zinc. But I doubted John Glenn knew this.

It reminded me of Mr. Snortland's musical chairs.
But there were enough chairs to go around, so no
McCarthy was left out.

Anne looked at the book in John Glenn's hand.

"How many conductors does it take to screw in a light bulb?" she asked.

"A conductor is a material that allows the flow of electricity," Ben said. "It is not a person. It cannot screw in a light bulb." Ben has no sense of humor.

Anne gave Ben a strange look and rolled her eyes. She turned back to John Glenn. "No one knows how many conductors it takes to screw in a light bulb because no one ever looks at the conductor. Get it?"

Mom was the only one who laughed.[23]

----

23   Don't worry if you don't get this joke. It is not very funny and it has nothing to do with electricity. It is about a different kind of conductor. Mom is in a choir, so she knows about music conductors, not electrical conductors. Apparently she doesn't look at her conductor.

8

Monday, 7:36 p.m.

I skipped Mom's nightly reading session in the boys' room. I wanted to do some of my own reading.

Well, not reading really. I just looked at the figures and sidebars in my library books. I was not doing too much actual reading. But that does not mean I wasn't learning.

I opened up *Fruity and Freaky Batteries*. I learned a number of important battery facts and recorded them in my notebook.

I studied these battery facts very carefully. Facts are important to scientists.

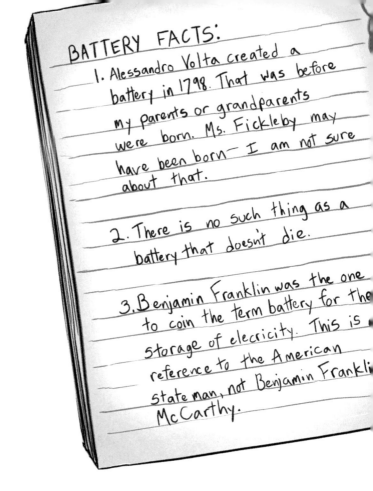

BATTERY FACTS:

1. Alessandro Volta created a battery in 1798. That was before my parents or grandparents were born. Ms. Fickleby may have been born — I am not sure about that.

2. There is no such thing as a battery that doesn't die.

3. Benjamin Franklin was the one to coin the term battery for the storage of elecricity. This is reference to the American state man, not Benjamin Frankli McCarthy.

I wanted to know all about batteries so I could understand electricity. And I wanted to understand more about electricity before I became principal for the day.

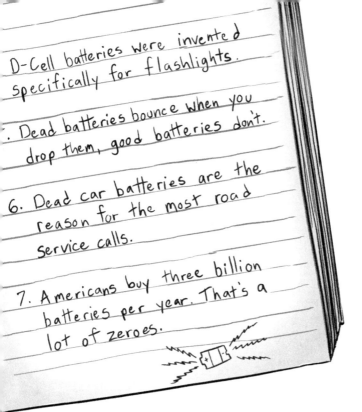

D-Cell batteries were invented specifically for flashlights.

. Dead batteries bounce when you drop them, good batteries don't.

6. Dead car batteries are the reason for the most road service calls.

7. Americans buy three billion batteries per year. That's a lot of zeroes.

But before that, I would have to win the arm-wrestling contest. I would have to learn to think like John Glenn. So I put down *Fruity and Freaky Batteries* and opened up *How Conductors Work*. I tried to figure out what John Glenn was reading before dinner. If only there was a book called *How John Glenn Works . . .*

9

Tuesday, 10:15 a.m.

The next day in PE, Mr. Swett had us do push-ups. Mr. Swett is our PE teacher. He is a former Navy SEAL.[24]

"Push-ups will strengthen your arms for the annual arm-wrestling contest!" he shouted. I could have told him that arm wrestling has nothing to do with strength. It is all about technique. But I decided to keep my mouth shut.

For good measure, Mr. Swett also had us run the mile. I am not sure how that would help us arm wrestle.

---

24   Navy SEALs are a special operations unit of the Navy. SEAL stands for Sea, Air, and Land Teams. So, I would think they would be called SALTs, but they're not.

As I was rounding the baseball field, I started to get a pain in my side. I am not cut out for running. I am better at observing.[25]

I ran past the window near the office hallway. I saw John Glenn waiting in the orange plastic chairs outside of Principal Cornforth's office.

---

25 These pains are also referred to as side stitches. They are common in beginning runners. If you haven't figured it out, PE is not my strongest subject.

That made me think about my hypothesis: *When the lights go out at the McCarthy house, someone gets into mischief.* But who was I trying to kid? John Glenn gets into mischief all the time.

Maybe the lights going out triggered all of John Glenn's sly ideas. Maybe my hypothesis should have been *When the lights go out at the McCarthy house, it will trigger a chain reaction.*

And this particular observation — John Glenn sitting outside the principal's office — was part of that chain reaction.

Then I thought of another reason to win the arm-wrestling contest. If I were principal for the day, I could figure out what John Glenn was up to! There wasn't a day that went by that John Glenn didn't visit the principal's office.

After PE, we went to reading class. Ms. Fickleby had to take a phone call. "I would like each of you to take out a book. Read quietly for ten minutes," she said.

Luckily, I had *How Conductors Work* in my backpack. I glanced at the pictures. I read the captions. I noticed how the copper wires were covered in rubber or plastic.

John Glenn came into the classroom. Ms. Fickleby didn't notice he was late. She was still on the phone.

"Why are those wires wrapped up?" whispered John Glenn. He was unusually interested in my book.

"So the electrons stay in the wires," I answered. "Why were you in the principal's office?"

"STEM team," he said. "Where do you get wires like that?"[26]

"You buy them at the store," I said. "And we don't have a STEM team."

"We have one now," he said. "How do you get electrons to come out of the wires?"

"I'm not sure. Maybe you need a battery," I said. "Why don't you ask someone on the STEM team?"

---

26 STEM stands for Science, Technology, Engineering, and Math. And for the record, Hilltop does NOT have a STEM team. And if they did, I would be on that team before John Glenn.

"We haven't studied electricity yet," he said. "What do you do with the battery?"

"You hook up the battery to the wires. That makes a circuit," I said.[27]

John Glenn smiled. He was up to something, and I was going to figure out what.

Ms. Fickleby hung up the phone. "John Glenn, here is a hall pass," she said. "Go down to Mr. Cornforth's office right away."

Maybe she *had* noticed him come in late. Maybe he was in trouble. I was pretty sure there was no STEM team. Whatever John Glenn was up to, Principal Cornforth was onto him too.

If I became principal for a day, I would figure out how John Glenn got away with so much. He was bound to get caught eventually, and I could find out John Glenn's plans before he got kicked out of Hilltop Elementary.

----
27   A circuit means that the wires go all the way around. Like in a circle. Or a square. Or a triangle, I guess. The point is that the wires have to go all the way around and back to where they started. Just keep reading. You'll figure it out before the end.

10

Tuesday, 3:35 p.m.

When we got to the house that afternoon, Mom was already home. She announced that we needed to run some errands. First we were going to the thrift shop.[28]

We were going to the thrift shop because Charlotte needed new jeans. Since I am the fourth oldest, I usually don't get any new clothes. A pair of Charlotte's jeans gets passed to Emily, then to Anne, and then to me. And by the time they get to me, they have holes and rips and stains.

---

28 The thrift shop is this place where you buy used stuff for really cheap. The McCarthys do a lot of shopping at the thrift shop. It's like a huge indoor garage sale. You can get a pair of jeans for one dollar. Or you might find some LEGOs or an old TV for five bucks.

After we got in the van, John Glenn asked me, "How many volts are in a car battery?"

"Why do you want to know?" I asked.

"I want to do something. I need to know how many volts it takes," he said.

A fight was breaking out in the third-row seat, and it was getting hard to have an electrical talk. A ride in a van with seven kids is never dull.

"What do you want to do?" I asked.

"I want to light a bulb," he said.

"Well then, the number of volts you would need would depend on how big the bulb is," I answered.

I thought about what I had read in my library books. The size of the battery doesn't matter. Power matters. But I was trying to hold back electrical information from John Glenn. You never know what kind of trouble that kid will get in with his imagination.

"Mom, can we go to the pet store after?" asked John Glenn.

"Why?" asked Mom.

"I want to look at the electric eels," said John Glenn.

"I don't think they have those, John Glenn," Mom answered.

"Do they have batteries at the thrift store?" he asked.

"No," said Mom as she gave him a strange look through the rearview mirror.

At the thrift store, I went to check out the electronics department. John Glenn was turning a lamp on and off. He saw me looking at him and tried to look casual. I tried to look casual too. I didn't want him to see that I was also interested in electricity.

"What exactly are you doing?" I asked. I opened and closed a waffle maker as I waited for John Glenn to answer.

Instead he asked, "Do you have five dollars?"

"Why?" I jiggled a knob on the top of an old camera.

"I was thinking that I could use the parts from this lamp," he said.

"For what?" I popped a toaster lever up and down.

"I want to make a circuit that turns on a light," he said.

"How?" I twirled the turntable on a record player.[29]

"You sound like Edison," he said.

"What?" shouted Edison from the next aisle. We saw Mom's head over the top of a rack of clothes and started to whisper.

"I don't have five dollars anyway," I said. And if I did, I wouldn't give it to John Glenn.

"Bummer," said John Glenn.

----

29   A record player is what your grandparents or maybe your great-grandparents used to listen to music. Really old music, like opera or marching band or disco.

11

Our trip to the thrift store gave me an idea. A good scientist needs to investigate ideas from time to time. So I headed down to the basement to do some research.

Our basement is not a nice place — you probably remember that from Chapter One. You wouldn't want to spend much time there.

Among the dust and spiders and Dad's old magazines, there are lots of boxes of junk and broken toys. I found a box with a toy race car track and some cars.

As I dug through the box, a spider crawled across my hand, and I let out a little scream. I covered my mouth, though, because I didn't want anyone to find me. Especially John Glenn.

I found some wires. I even found Charlotte's old Easy-Bake Oven — the one that she would never let anyone else touch.

I opened the oven. There was a small light bulb inside — and that gave me another idea. Maybe I could make a circuit and light a bulb. Then maybe I could figure out why our lights went out during the storm. Maybe I could do an experiment with electricity.

I quickly put my stash in a cardboard box and ran up to my room. I stashed the box under my bed before anyone saw me.[30]

---

30   And by anyone, I mean John Glenn.

12

Wednesday, 8:30 a.m.

The next day in Mrs. Stickler's homeroom, Mr. Cornforth coughed through the loud speaker. He had another announcement.

"In order to prepare for the annual arm-wrestling contest," he began, "students in grades three through five will have PE every day for the rest of the week."

Great.

When we went to PE a little later, Mr. Swett had us warm up with thirty burpees.[31]

---

31   Burpees were invented by an American guy named Royal Burpee. Mr. Swett loves burpees. I don't pretend to be an expert on the matter, but this Royal guy was a royal pain for the students at Hilltop.

Next came another run around the baseball field.

Finally, Mr. Swett announced that we were going back inside to the gym. He wanted to show us something. The PTA had bought us a new arm-wrestling table.

As we walked in, I thought I saw John Glenn slipping out the exit on the other side of the gym. What was he doing? Maybe he was spying on the arm-wrestling practice so he could pick up some tips. I needed to ask John Glenn how he got away with this. Maybe I could learn something from a second grader.

The arm-wrestling table was fancy. There were grips for your left hand and cushions for your right. When you slammed the other person's arm down, they wouldn't get hurt.

"All right, line up by height!" shouted Mr. Swett. Great. I am the tallest in the class. I tried to slouch. "McCarthy!"

"Yes, Mr. Swett?" I said.

"Get to the end of the line," he said. "We are going to start with the shortest."

Bummer. That meant I was right next to Randy Studley.

The two shortest in the class arm wrestled first. Emma beat Henry. And so it went until it was my turn to arm wrestle Randy.

Randy smiled. "This is going to be easy," he said.

We clasped our hands. His palms were sweaty. I focused on the correct angle between my bicep and forearm.

"Go!" said Mr. Swett. Randy started to tilt my arm down. I struggled. I thought about technique. I recovered and tilted Randy's arm the other way. Suddenly Randy slammed my hand down.

Mr. Swett said, "McCarthy, I can't wait to see the rematch at the assembly on Friday. You'd better work on your technique!"

13

Wednesday, 3:45 p.m.

We walked in the front door after school and headed straight to the kitchen.

"Who wants to help peel and cut fruit for the fruit salad?" Dad asked.

"I have homework," Charlotte said sweetly, "otherwise, I would be glad to help." She turned and walked out of the kitchen. Emily and Anne followed her.

"Dad, do you have any extra batteries?" John Glenn asked.

"What for?" Dad asked.

"Our flashlight is burnt out," said John Glenn.

"I think we are out of batteries," said Dad. "But did you know that you can make a battery out of a piece of fruit? Tell you what. You help me peel these oranges, and I will explain how you can make citrus fruit into a battery."

John Glenn and the boys helped Dad with his fruit. I started to help, even though that smell made me think of fruity Mr. Snortland.

"Now take this lemon . . . ," Dad began.

"Is there electricity inside?" asked John Glenn.

"Well, no," Dad said. "The acid in the lemon is an electrolyte. Batteries require three things — two electrodes and one electrolyte."[32]

"What about electrons?" I asked.

"You're right, Curious," said Dad. "One electrode wants electrons more than the other. That's why they move."

"So can you use a lemon to light a flashlight?" asked John Glenn.

Dad laughed. "You might need a lot more fruit for that. But good use of your imagination!"[33]

----

32   Dad likes to use big words. You don't need to know this stuff. But if you are curious, you might want to check out a book on how batteries work. Check the nonfiction section.

33   Actually, I learned later that you can create more power by adding more electrodes instead of lemons. But in the end, I am glad John Glenn didn't know that.

When we were done with the fruit it was time to arm wrestle. Dad called Anne back to the kitchen.

"Let's see how you do left-handed," Dad said.

"Will they let me arm wrestle with my left hand?" I asked.

"Maybe," said Dad. "It doesn't hurt to ask. And that will give you an advantage."

"Why?" asked Edison.

"Only ten percent of the population is left-handed," said Dad. "That means lefties get a lot more practice competing against righties."

Dad made Anne put up her left hand. I won easily. I beat a fifth grader! And this gave me an idea. Maybe I could win that arm-wrestling contest by using my left arm.[34]

I smiled. I was starting to think like John Glenn.

---

34 Some scientists think that left-handers have an advantage in lots of one-on-one sports like tennis and arm wrestling. I had spent this week practicing right-handed. I bet Randy wasn't practicing left-handed.

14

Wednesday, 7:00 p.m.

After dinner that night, I walked upstairs. I wanted to check out the box of stuff that I had brought up from the basement the night before. On the way, I observed the pictures Mom had put on the wall. Not in any orderly pattern, like Dad would have done. They were here and there. The frames were silver, gold, black, and brown.[35]

They were mostly school pictures. But there were plenty of baby pictures of Charlotte. After Charlotte, each kid had fewer and fewer pictures on the wall.

----
35   They probably came from the thrift store.

That is, until John Glenn arrived.

There were at least six baby pictures of him. They must have been excited for the first boy. In one picture, he wore a pale blue sweater and matching shorts. With his blond hair and blue eyes, every adult thought he was an angel.[36]

When I got to the top of the stairs, I quietly walked down to the boys' door and peeked inside. John Glenn was sitting on the floor with a bunch of wires. He didn't notice me. It looked like he was trying to put together a circuit.[37]

I also saw that he had both my library books sitting on the floor next to him. *How Conductors Work* was lying open on one side of him and *Fruity and Freaky Batteries* was lying open on the other side.

I am the scientist in this family! What the heck was John Glenn doing? Those were my library books!

---

36 Every adult was wrong.
37 A complete circuit is a closed circuit. Not an open circuit. Electrons will not flow if the circuit is not closed. That means the wires are all connected in a circle. Or another shape. You must remember this from Chapter Eight.

Then I noticed he had my box from the basement too. He must have been using the wires that I had found.

"What are you doing with my stuff?!" I shouted as I ran into the room.

John Glenn looked up and tried to move in front of the wires. "Too late," I said as I grabbed my books. "What is the circuit for?"

When he moved in front of the wires, I saw the Easy-Bake Oven.

He looked at me with big eyes. He tilted his head. He smiled. He batted his eyelashes.

I knew this look. He used it on Mom and Dad all the time. I've even seen him use it on Ms. Fickleby. He said, "I could use some help."

"You never ask for help," I said suspiciously.

"I volunteered to help with the arm-wrestling contest," he said. "I wanted to make a light that will light up when the winner pins the loser's arm down."

"Well," I said, "you'll need a battery."

But I wasn't convinced that he was telling me the whole story. Even though I was really mad, I tried to stay calm. Scientists have to be impartial.[38]

"We don't have any new batteries," he said.

"Can't you ask for a battery at school?" I asked.

He didn't look in my direction. I could tell he was trying to think up a good answer.

"Mr. Cornforth said that there was a fire at the battery factory," he said.

"Sure," I said. John Glenn and I stared at each other. Neither of us was going to budge.

"We have lemons," said Ben, walking into the room. Ben was studying the circuit.

"But you heard Dad," I said. "You'd need more fruit. I'll tell you what, John Glenn. I will help you make a circuit. But you're going to need a light bulb too."

----
38   Impartial means you treat your rivals – or brothers – fairly. You stay calm and don't clobber them with an Easy-Bake Oven.

"Here's one," said Ben. He was digging inside the Easy-Bake Oven.[39]

"Okay," I said to John Glenn. "I will help you. But you have to find the battery."

---

39 He is named after Benjamin Franklin, after all. Benjamin Franklin didn't discover lightning or "invent" electricity, but he was known to shock his friends at dinner parties . . . though probably not with an Easy-Bake Oven.

"Okay," he said.

"AND you also have to help me figure out a way to win the arm-wrestling contest," I added. "You might be able to convince Mr. Cornforth to let me arm wrestle left-handed." I figured John Glenn was the best kid at Hilltop Elementary at figuring out how to get away with things.

With John Glenn's help, I had a better chance of winning that contest. That meant I had a better chance of becoming principal for the day. And I would have a better chance of finding out how the electricity at the school worked . . . and how John Glenn worked.

We set to work creating a circuit that would light a bulb.

15

Thursday, 8:05 a.m.

We knew it as soon as we walked through the front door of the school. One of us would have Mr. Snortland as a substitute.

You could smell that aftershave at the front door. You could smell it in the cafeteria. You could smell it in the bathrooms. You could smell it through the whole school.

I was relieved when I walked into homeroom and saw Mrs. Stickler.

My relief didn't last long. At gym time, we found out Mr. Snortland was subbing for Mr. Swett.

He decided that we didn't need to do push-ups or run the mile — we needed to learn how to square dance.[40]

---

40   Square dancing is something you should ask your parents about. It is a dance with four couples standing in a square. One couple on each side. Because a square has four sides . . . but I guess you already knew that.

We started dancing. I had to breathe through my mouth so I wouldn't gag from Mr. Snortland's aftershave. Mr. Snortland called, "Round your partner! DO-SI-DO!" He had us do all kinds of fancy moves.

While I was swinging my partner 'round and 'round, I saw John Glenn walk into the other end of the gym.

"Come join in, son!" called Mr. Snortland.

"I can't. I am with the STEM team. Mr. Cornforth sent me in to work on the arm-wrestling table," said John Glenn.

I kept watching John Glenn. He must have found a battery for the circuit we made. He set the cardboard box on the floor.

I wondered if I could get away with telling Mr. Snortland that I needed to help the STEM team too. Maybe that would get me out of dancing. I thought about this as I was swinging 'round and 'round.

"Slow down," called Mr. Snortland. "Dancing is all about technique!" He sounded like Dad.

But dancing technique involved touching boys. So I was kind of grossed out. I was not about to slow down so that we'd have to touch for longer. I would much rather be putting together a circuit than dancing with boys. Could I tell Mr. Snortland that I was on the STEM team too?

John Glenn unloaded the wires. Then he moved in front of the table. He set down a big grocery bag.

He put his hand into the bag. He pulled something out. He was turned away, so I could not see what it was.

"Swing your partner, 'round and 'round!" called Mr. Snortland.

We had just switched partners and Randy Studley hooked my elbow. He swung hard.

I flew across the floor and smashed right into Mr. Snortland. Yuck!

It was too late to join the STEM team. I am just not as tricky as John Glenn.

16

Thursday, 6:00 p.m.

Mom rushed in, and we sat down to dinner. She sniffed and then looked at each of us. Her nose scrunched up.

"What is that?" she asked.

"What?" asked Edison.

"That smell," she said.[41]

"What smell?" asked Edison.

"That awful smell," said Mom.

"How's arm-wrestling practice going?" Dad interrupted.

----
41   Have I mentioned Mom's super-human smelling abilities? She can smell a dirty sock from out on the sidewalk.

"Fine," I said.

"John Glenn," said Dad, "do you want a few
more tips?"

"No, that's okay," said John Glenn. "I think I've
got the technique down."

"Second graders aren't even part of the contest,"
I said. "But I need a few more tips."

Dad smiled at that, but Mom was still sniffing about. Before Dad could say anything, Mom said, "It smells like spoiled fruit and hair spray. John Glenn, is that you? It smells just like the aftershave of an old substitute teacher we had as kids," said Mom.

"It's Curious!" said John Glenn. "She danced with Mr. Snortland!"

I pinched him under the table so my parents couldn't see.

"OUCH!" he shouted way too loudly.

I got sent upstairs to shower. No one could stand the fruity aftershave smell.

17

Thursday, 7:57 p.m.

Later that night, Mom went to the boys' room to read. She always reads in the boys' room because Edison always falls asleep before she finishes. Tonight, she read *Frankenstein*.[42]

She must have finished reading it and decided it was okay to read to the kids. My parents read all the books and watch all the movies first. Just to make sure that everything is appropriate.

John Glenn listened closely. Mom got to the part that said:

---

42   *Frankenstein* is a book by Mary Shelley. It's one of Mom's favorites. When your mother is a college English professor, you have very interesting bedtime reading.

I eagerly inquired of my father

the nature and origin of thunder

and lightning. He replied, "Electricity."

John Glenn's eyes sparkled. It looked as if there really could be a tiny light bulb in his head.

Mom finished reading and tucked the boys in. Charlotte, Emily, Anne, and I moved toward our room.

Dad passed us in the hallway and said, "Tomorrow is the arm-wrestling contest. Anne, Curious, and John Glenn need their sleep!"

"John Glenn is not in the contest," I said.

Dad just smiled.

18

Friday, 1:00 a.m.[43]

I woke up suddenly, thinking that I heard something. Deciding to check it out, I tiptoed to the hall. I could see a light under the boys' door. I crept down the hall and listened.

"Touch it!" said John Glenn.

"No. You touch it," said Ben.

"I'm not going to touch it, you touch it!" said John Glenn.

"I'm not going to touch it," said Ben.

---

43   Yes, you read that right. It was one o'clock a.m. That means really, really, really early in the morning. You don't need to know the rest of this, so you can stop reading if you want. The initials a.m. stand for *ante meridiem*. Those are Latin words. They mean *before midday* – way before midday. You're still reading. It was just an hour after midnight.

I reached for the handle. I slowly, slowly turned the knob.

"CURIOUS!" said Dad. "What are you doing out of bed?" Dad was just coming up the stairs. Why was he up this late? I turned to point to the light under John Glenn's door, but it was gone.

"Sleepwalking," I said.[44]

----
44   Up to 30 percent of children sleepwalk. I could be one of them.

19

Friday, 7:03 a.m.

I stopped at the boys' room on my way to breakfast.
The boys weren't around. I saw the cardboard box
was sitting on the floor. There were no wires inside.
Just a book. It was John Glenn's library book, *All
Charged Up!*

I noticed there was a bookmark in the book. It
was actually a little folded-up piece of a magazine.

I unfolded it carefully. The page was all worn
out and a little ripped around the edges. It said,
"Boy's Life." I couldn't read the date, but it had to
be pretty old.

It had all kinds of practical joke stuff that you could order by mail. Like:

X-ray glasses.

Mini spy cameras.

Silent dog whistles.

Whoopie cushions.

And . . .

Joy buzzers.

Under the joy buzzers, it said, "How to make a joy buzzer to shock your friends. Wind up and wear like a ring! A GREAT GAG! New and Improved!"

The Easy-Bake Oven was sitting on Ben's bed.

I opened up the oven. The light bulb was still there. Whatever John Glenn was doing, it had nothing to do with a light for the arm-wrestling table.

A light bulb turned on in my head.[45]

On my way to the kitchen, I stuck my tongue out at John Glenn's adorable baby picture.

I wanted to know what he was doing up in the middle of the night. I walked into the kitchen to confront him.

"Where's John Glenn?" I asked Dad.

"He had some equipment to take to school. For the STEM team. Your Mom took him in the van on her way to work. He sure is working hard on that STEM team," Dad said proudly.

Sure, I thought. *The school doesn't even have a STEM team.*

----

45   OK. Not really. That is just an idiom. We've been through this before, haven't we? I bet you are wondering how I know all about idioms. Mom teaches English, remember?

But John Glenn and I had a deal. I didn't know what he was up to, but I couldn't snitch on him. He was going to help me win this contest.

"What were you guys doing last night?" I whispered to Ben.

"Nothing," he answered.

"I know what you're up to," I said. "Where did you get a battery?"

"We don't have any batteries," Ben said.

20

Friday, 1:15 p.m.

After lunch, everyone was buzzing with excitement.
Mr. Swett was back and we would all get out of
reading class to go to the arm-wrestling contest.

I observed the boys all flexing their muscles.
Randy Studley was smiling and joking with the others.

"Watch me beat all the fifth graders," he said. "I've
been doing one-armed push-ups!" He flexed his arm
again and looked right at me.

I smiled. I would win this contest. I would become
principal for the day.[46]

----
46   Because I was pretty sure that Randy hadn't been doing one-armed push-ups with
his left arm.

When we arrived at Ms. Fickleby's class, John Glenn was missing. He probably has Ms. Fickleby convinced that Hilltop has a STEM team.

"Ladies in one line, gentlemen in the other," Ms. Fickleby said. Did I mention Ms. Fickleby is old-fashioned?

I was at the end of the girls' line. Randy was at the end of the boys'. We walked down to the gym. Randy flexed his muscles most of the way.

When we got to the gym, John Glenn was standing by the door. Mr. Swett was standing proudly at the new arm-wrestling table. His left hand was stroking one of the metal handles.

I smelled fruit and started looking around for Mr. Snortland. Apparently, I wasn't the only one who smelled fruit. I heard Mr. Swett ask Mr. Cornforth if there was a substitute today. He shook his head.

"Take your seats!" Mr. Cornforth shouted into his microphone. "We are ready to start with the third graders." We quickly shuffled to the bleachers, down our row, and sat down.

The third graders were lined up at the side of the gym. Mr. Swett was still holding one handle of the arm-wrestling table gently with his left hand. And smiling at it. Like it was a new baby or something.

Mr. Cornforth said into the microphone, "Mr. Swett, will you please announce the rules of the contest?"

Then Mr. Cornforth leaned against the table, grabbing the other metal handle with his left hand. He reached his right hand across the table to give Mr. Swett the microphone. Mr. Swett grabbed the microphone with his right hand. Suddenly, Mr. Cornforth and Mr. Swett screamed like two little kids on a roller coaster.[47]

47   Or two middle-aged men on a roller coaster. Or two middle-aged men who were just shocked by a joy buzzer because they completed the electrical circuit.

A watermelon, three oranges, and a grapefruit tumbled out from beneath the arm-wrestling table. The watermelon split open with a splash. Wires stuck out all over the pile of smashed fruit.

My eyes darted toward the door. John Glenn was gone.

And soon Mr. Swett was gone too, thundering down the hall after him.

Due to all the mischief that John Glenn created, we did not get to finish the arm-wrestling contest. First the janitor was called in for the cleanup. Then Mr. Cornforth had to go back to his office and call Dad about John Glenn. Then Mr. Swett had to catch his breath before he could announce the rules . . . standing a safe distance away from the arm-wrestling table.

In the end, only the third graders got to wrestle. Mr. Swett said the rest of us would have to wait for next year.

21

Saturday, 8:00 a.m.

I walked down to breakfast early. Dad was flipping pancakes. Mom was sitting at the table with an industrial-sized cup of coffee. They both had smiles on their faces.

I scanned the room trying to figure out what made them so happy. Did we get a housekeeper?

Then I noticed John Glenn on his knees in the corner. He was scrubbing the floor — with an orange toothbrush.

Hypothesis: confirmed. When the lights go out at the McCarthy house, someone gets into mischief.

And in this case, someone also gets grounded and has to scrub the floors with a toothbrush. The toilets were probably next.

Conclusions

Scientists like to observe. And here's something I learned from my observations. The next time Dad tells us to use our imaginations, he should probably give a warning. Like:

DON'T TRY THIS AT HOME!
ADULT SUPERVISION REQUIRED!
NOT RECOMMENDED FOR CHILDREN UNDER 10!

Scientists also like to make conclusions. Here are my conclusions for the week:

- John Glenn has proved that in science, imagination might be as important as intelligence. John Glenn did get me more time to work on my technique. I have another year before the next arm-wrestling contest.
- Dad should have made some fruitcake with that leftover fruit.

- If I ever get to be principal for a day, I will form the Hilltop STEM team. That might be the only way I will learn about electricity at school.
- Thunder always comes with lightning.[48]

---

48   Just ask Mr. Swett. Or John Glenn.

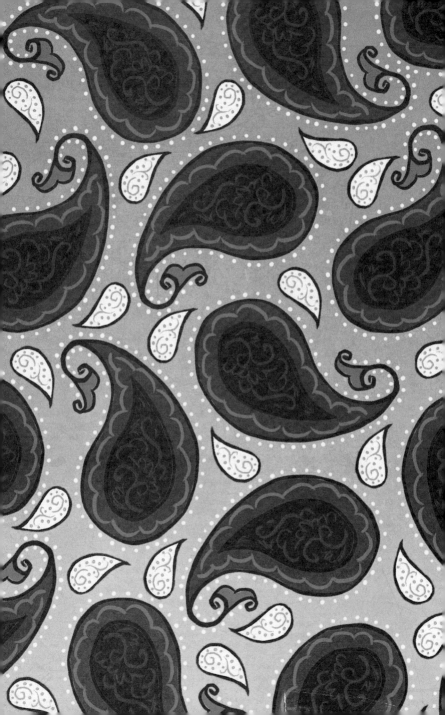

SCIENCE STUNT
FUN WITH STATIC ELECTRICITY

If you get stuck inside with your six brothers and sisters, you might want to try this. It is more fun than making shocks by dragging your stocking feet on the carpet . . . well, that's fun too. So you should try both . . . even if you don't have six brothers and sisters.

What you need:

- Blown-up balloons
- Plastic grocery bags[49]
- A wool cloth or a head of hair[50]
- Scissors

What you do:

1. Cut little strips of the plastic bag (about the size of a ruler).
2. Rub the plastics strips on the cloth or head of hair for about 20 seconds.
3. Rub a balloon on the cloth or head of hair too.
4. Hold the balloon in your hands.
5. Now gently place the plastic strip about 10 centimeters above the balloon. The plastic strip should float above the balloon. See how long you can keep it floating!

The balloon and the plastic bag are both negatively charged. This means that they repel, or push away from, each other. Kind of like me and Randy Studley.

For more science stunts, visit www.torychristie.com

---

49   You should feel good about this experiment. You are recycling!
50   Either your own or maybe a little brother's.

 GLOSSARY

atom (AT-uhm)–the tiniest part of an element that has all the properties of that element

circuit (SUR-kit)–the complete path that an electrical current can flow

conductor (kuhn-DUHK-tur)–a substance that allows heat, electricity, or sound to travel through it

copper (KOP-ur)–a reddish brown metal that conducts heat and electricity well

electrode (i-LEK-trode)–a point through which an electric current can flow into or out of a device or substance

electrolyte (i-LEK-truh-lite)–a soluble substance that conducts electricity

electron (i-LEK-tron)–a tiny particle that moves around the nucleus of an atom

evidence (EV-uh-dehnss)–information and facts that help prove something

hypothesis (hye-POTH-uh-siss)–a prediction that can be tested about how a scientific investigation or experiment will turn out

mischief (MISS-chif)–behavior that may cause annoyance or harm to others

observation (ob-zur-VAY-shuhn)–an act of gathering information by noting facts or occurrences

research (REE-surch)–study or investigation to learn new facts or to solve a problem

shock (SHOK)–the effect of an electric current passing through someone's body

static electricity (STAT-ik i-lek-TRISS-uh-tee)–electricity that builds up in an object and stays there. Static electricity can be produced when one object rubs against another

volt (VOHLT)–a unit for measuring the force of an electrical current of the stored power of a battery

FURTHER INQUIRIES

1. Curious wanted to be principal for a day. Explain why. What would you do if you were principal for a day?

2. Curious concludes that in science, imagination may be as important as intelligence. What does she mean by that?

3. Do you think John Glenn got in trouble at school too? If so, what do you think his punishment was?

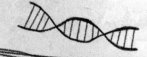

RECORD YOUR FINDINGS

1. Curious is named after the scientist Marie Curie. Research Curie and write a short report about her.

2. Create a poster for the school's arm-wrestling contest. Be sure to cover the who, what, when, and where, using details from the book.

3. Write a newspaper article about what happened at the school's arm-wrestling contest. Include quotes from Mr. Cornforth and Mr. Swett.

REFERENCES

Scientists should tell readers where they got their information. We call these "References." Scientists do this in case readers want to do more research.

MRS. MCCARTHY'S AND MS. FICKLEBY'S REFERENCE LIST

Frankenstein: or, the Modern Prometheus by Mary Shelley[51]

What's the Attraction? by Elizabeth Raum

Maglev Trains by Louise and Richard Spilsbury

How Conductors Work by Victoria G. Christensen

All Charged Up! by Jennifer Boothroyd

Magnets, Monsters, and Mummies by Frank E. Stein

Fruity and Freaky Batteries by North Snortland[52]

----

51   Prometheus was a god in Greek mythology. In those Greek stories, Prometheus created humans and taught them things like how to make fire . . . this is a bit complicated. Don't try to read this book yourself. Go find a grown-up.

52   These last two are not real books. I made them up. I can do that because this is fiction.

ABOUT THE AUTHOR

Tory Christie is a real scientist by day and secretly writes children's books at night. When it is light outside, she studies rocks and water. After dark, she writes silly science stories that kids and grown-ups can laugh about. Although she grew up in a large family, her family was nothing like the McCarthys — honestly. The McCarthys are completely fictional — really. Tory Christie lives in Fargo, North Dakota, with her medium-sized family.

ABOUT THE ILLUSTRATOR

As a professional illustrator and designer, Mina Price has a particular love for book illustration and character design, or basically any project that allows her to draw interesting people in cool outfits. Mina graduated from the Maryland Institute College of Art with a BFA in Illustration. When she is not drawing, Mina can frequently be found baking things with lots of sugar or getting way too emotional over a good book.

MAKE MORE DISCOVERIES WITH CURIOUS!

FIND:

Videos & Contests
Games & Puzzles
Heroes & Villains
Authors & Illustrators

www.CAPSTONEKIDS.com

Find cool websites and more books just like this one at www.FACTHOUND.com. Just type in the book I.D. 9781515816447 and you're ready to go!